MindReader
THE CRYSTAL

Pete Johnson

1ˢᵗ Edition
1ˢᵗ reprint

telos
EDITORA

Direitos de impressão desta edição no Brasil: TELOS EDITORA

Telos Editora Ltda.
Rua Caio Graco, 764 – Vila Romana
05044-000 – São Paulo – SP
Tel. (11) 2373-5007
www.teloseditora.com.br

Edição Original
ISBN: 978-1-78270-303-7

Cover design by Patrick Knowles
Illustrations by Anthony Smith

Text copyright © 2018 Pete Johnson
This edition copyright © Award Publications Limited

The right of Pete Johnson to be identified as the author of this work has been asserted in accordance with the Copyright, Designs and Patents Act 1988.

All rights reserved. No part of this publication may be reproduced or utilised in any form or by any means electronic or mechanical, including photocopying, recording, or by any information storage and retrieval system now known or hereafter invented, without the prior written permission of the publisher.

First published by Award Publications Limited 2018

Published by Award Publications Limited,
The Old Riding School, Welbeck,
Worksop, S80 3LR

www.awardpublications.co.uk

Dados Internacionais de Catalogação na Publicação (CIP)

J68m
    Johnson, Pete;
    The crystal: Mind Reader / Pete Johnson; illustrated by Anthony Smith. – São Paulo : Telos, 2020.

    ISBN: 978-65-86106-01-5

    1. Children's literature – 2. Readers. I. Smith, Anthony. II. Title.

CDD: 028.5

Índices para catálogo sistemático:

1. Children's literature   028.5
2. Readers   028.5

ASSOCIADO **CBL**
Câmara Brasileira do Livro

Rosa Cleide Marques – Bibliotecária – CRB-8/878

Printed in Brazil - February 2024

*The book is dedicated, with gratitude,
to the literary agent George Greenfield,
who gave me so much encouragement
when I first started writing.*

Chapter One

The Dangerous Gift

I know what you're thinking. In fact, I know every one of your secrets. But don't be scared of me. By myself I have no special powers at all.

I'm Matt, nicknamed Spud because my nose looks a bit like a potato.

And I'm the most ordinary boy you'll ever meet. Or I was until ... now I'm jumping ahead. And I want to tell you everything, just as it happened.

It all started when I was left something in Mrs Jameson's will. I was totally amazed. I'd never been left anything in a will before.

Mrs Jameson was a very old lady. I first visited her with a harvest festival gift from our school.

She frowned at me. "None of it looks very fresh – and bananas give me indigestion."

"Me too," I grinned. "I can't stop burping for days."

She looked at me suddenly, and a faint smile crossed her face. "I suppose I could try to eat some of it. You'd better come in."

We sat in her kitchen. She poured me a glass of orange juice. Then I asked her if she liked living on her own.

"Yes, of course I like it," she snapped. "Other people only cause problems. You can't trust a single one of them." She glared at me. I hastily changed the subject.

Around her neck hung a crystal on a long silver chain. It caught my eye right away. She saw me looking at it.

"This crystal was left to me by my great aunt, who took a shine to me. A strange woman – used to call herself a wizard. You didn't know there were any female wizards, did you?"

Actually, I didn't know many male wizards either – not personally, anyway.

She leaned forward. "This crystal is priceless. But no one else knows my crystal's true worth – and that's how it must stay. Otherwise I'd never have a moment's peace."

She was exaggerating now. She must be.

Still, I must admit the crystal fascinated me. Maybe because there were flashes of so many colours in it.

"I love all the colours you can see," I said, "especially the sky blue at the centre." Then I added hastily, "It is blue, isn't it?"

She looked puzzled by my question, so I thought I'd better explain. "I'm what they call colour-deficient. I can see every single colour – I just see it in different ways. So I might see red as brown and brown as red. Blue and purple are pretty confusing too. That's why I asked."

"The crystal is blue in the centre, just as you said," she interrupted. Her eyes were blue too, and they were staring intently at me.

"Oh good, because sometimes I can make embarrassing mistakes. I went into a pet shop once and asked for the yellow hamster."

For the first time she gave a wheezy laugh, then said slowly, "You just see in your own world of colour, that's all. I expect my crystal is more beautiful in your eyes than anyone else's." I really liked the way she said that. She made me feel sort of special.

After that I visited her almost every day. We sat in her kitchen talking about practically everything. But then she became ill. She had pneumonia. She didn't want to leave her home but the doctor insisted. She'd only been in hospital for a couple of days when she died quite suddenly. She'd done that just to spite the doctor. That's what I told myself to try to cheer myself up.

I thought about her a lot over the next few days.

Then I discovered she'd left her precious crystal to me. She'd written me a letter too. On the envelope she'd put: STRICTLY PRIVATE – FOR MATTHEW COLLINS ONLY. I'm not sure why, but my hands shook as I opened the envelope.

Inside was her letter to me. Her handwriting was very shaky and difficult to read. Finally I made out:

Dear Matthew, I am leaving you my most valuable possession in gratitude for all those enjoyable hours we spent talking together. I do not want anyone else to discover how special my crystal is – ONLY YOU. But, Matthew, you must keep the secret and you must be careful, because my gift can be VERY DANGEROUS. As you will discover ...

This was followed by some squiggles, which I couldn't read.

I leant closer, trying to somehow read the final words. I had to know what Mrs Jameson meant about my crystal being very dangerous. It just didn't make any sense.

Then my mum peeked over my shoulder at the letter. "Poor thing," she said. "She was probably wandering in her mind when she wrote that. I expect she just wanted to make sure you took care of her gift."

But I didn't think that was true. Mrs Jameson's mind was as sharp as a pin right to the end. No, she was trying to tell me something about the crystal, something incredibly important.

But what?

Chapter Two

Secrets of the Crystal

I put the crystal on a keyring. I wore it to school on a loop on my belt. Even some of the teachers admired it.

After school, the crystal sat on the telly in my bedroom. When the sun came down, the crystal would shine all these different colours onto my wall, blue, pinkish-red, green, yellow. Then it did seem like a magic crystal. I thought of Mrs Jameson's great aunt, the wizard. Did she cast spells with this crystal? Maybe she turned people into slugs.

I wouldn't have minded turning Finn into a slug.

He's a new boy at our school who just loves himself. He's always showing off about his house – or how he's got more friends online than anyone else in the entire universe.

Actually, he's a real turnip-head. I mean, he's bottom of the year in maths. But not even that bothers him, he is so super-confident. I sort of envied his confidence, but I hated it as well. Especially the way he smirked around school like a cat that's not only swallowed all his cream, but all of yours too.

So just messing about, I picked up my crystal, closed my eyes and said, "Magic crystal turn Finn into a slug and never, ever turn him back."

I was only fooling around and I never expected anything to happen.

But something did all right.

The crystal suddenly started getting warmer.

It was like when you put your hand on a radiator that has just been switched on. You can feel the heat stealing up your fingers, can't you?

Well, it was the same with my crystal. And the crystal went on getting hotter, until in the end it seemed to be burning into my hands. I wasn't able to hold it any more. I had to let it drop onto my bed.

For a few seconds my fingers were still tingling. I couldn't believe how hot that crystal had become. I shivered with the shock.

I gave the crystal a quick prod. It was cold again. Yet as soon as I picked it up, exactly the same thing happened – the crystal got warm, and then after thirty-four seconds (yeah, I timed it) it became so hot I had to let it go.

But how weird was that?

I was tempted to run downstairs and tell Mum and Dad. But Alison, my older sister and my mortal enemy, was also downstairs. She'd already cast envious eyes on my crystal, saying how it was wasted on me.

And some words from Mrs Jameson's note rushed into my head. "You must keep the secret."

I'd never heard of a crystal that could get hot all by itself. That would certainly make it very valuable.

But Mrs Jameson hadn't just written 'valuable', she'd put 'very dangerous' as well.

I still didn't understand that. Then I suddenly

thought — what if the crystal could put spells on people too? What if one second Finn is posing about by his pool and the next he's slithering around as a slug?

I'd love to see his parents' faces when this slug starts chattering to them, claiming to be their marvellous son.

Of course, I was only messing about. Finn would be back at school tomorrow, wouldn't he?

Chapter Three

A Tremendous Discovery

But next morning, Finn wasn't at school. My hopes began to rise. And I wasn't at all ashamed that I'd turned him into a slug. Trust me, he deserved it.

Then at break time, very disappointingly, he appeared — that so annoying grin plastered all over his face as usual. Today he was wearing his new green designer-label shirt. He looked like a long processed pea in it. To make matters worse, he was talking to Emma.

Despite what you may have heard, Emma is not my girlfriend. Dream on! She is a mate though. My best mate to be exact.

Maybe you think that's a bit unusual. But she's been my best mate for nearly a year now.

At first I'd just spotted her at school – she's dead pretty and very friendly. I'd also see her taking her pet spaniel, Bess, for a walk. She always grinned at me while I struggled to think of something, *anything*, to say to her – and I'm not normally as shy as that – but I never could say anything even vaguely intelligible.

Until the day Bess went missing.

"I only left the front door open for one tiny second," Emma told me, "and the next thing I knew, she'd gone. And the thing is, Bess is a total wimp and not brave at all. She badly needs someone to look after her—"

"Don't worry," I interrupted, "I'll find her for you. Leave it to me." No superhero could have sounded more determined.

And guess what? I did find Bess. She was sniffing about in someone's bin and when I called her, she immediately followed me back to Emma's house. It was dead easy actually. But Emma treated me, well, exactly like a superhero

– of course I lapped that up. Then her parents insisted I stay for tea.

And that's when all my shyness rushed back. Did I mention Emma's very pretty? But then I noticed she kept glancing at a football match on the telly.

"You like football, don't you?" I said.

"Thought I'd only like netball, did you?" she replied with heavy sarcasm. "Whenever a girl shows an interest in football, why do all boys' chins hit the ground?"

"My chin's just fine," I replied. "I bet you know far more about football than me anyway."

And she really did. But then she'd gone to her first football match with her dad when she was only four.

"What team do you support?" she asked me suddenly.

"Spurs," I began.

Her eyes lit up. "So do I!"

That was so lucky, as she was a massive fan. She proudly showed me her Spurs calendar, Spurs torch and four Spurs shirts.

Then her dad offered to take us both to a

Spurs game. I tell you, it's so much better than watching it on the telly, for when you're there you're a real part of it. Now her dad was hoping to get us tickets for one of the biggest matches of the season – Spurs v Arsenal. I was really looking forward to seeing that with Emma.

Only, would you believe it, Finn is a massive Spurs fan too. He's always talking about them with Emma. And tons of other stuff too. She claims she doesn't really like Finn at all. But I have this horrible feeling she's far more impressed by him than she lets on.

That's why I decided to tell Emma about my crystal. After all, my crystal was way more exciting than anything Finn could boast about. In fact, my crystal was probably the only one of its kind.

I planned to tell her at lunchtime.

I stood waiting for Emma in the corner of the playground where we usually meet up.

I wanted to check the crystal was still working. I held it and nothing seemed to be happening. My heart sank. Maybe it only worked at night. Out of the corner of my eye I saw Finn walking towards me. He was the last person I wanted to talk to now. I deliberately looked away.

Then heat started to surge through it again. I let out a great sigh of relief. In the back of my head I could hear Mrs Jameson whisper, "You must keep the secret." I felt a stab of guilt. But I would swear Emma to secrecy and I wouldn't tell anyone else. Not ever.

Then I heard another voice whisper:

Great that Emma's dad has good seats for the Spurs v Arsenal match! I bet she takes me not Spud this time. I'm a much bigger fan than him. He only pretends to follow Spurs.

I recognised the voice instantly. It was Finn. I jumped around, thinking he was right behind me — that was how close he sounded. But in fact he was still a couple of metres away from me.

I let go of the crystal.

He strolled towards me, grinning. "Waiting for Emma, are you?"

He said this so casually I could only stutter,

"Y—Yes." Then he gave me this big friendly wave and he was gone.

I stared after him. I couldn't believe the way he'd blurted all that out to me and then acted so cool. He must be very sure of himself.

I was extremely uneasy now. And for the moment, I forgot about my crystal. Instead, I let Emma know what Finn had said. She was totally amazed. "I just happened to mention to him that my dad had got the tickets, that's all. I was going to tell you too."

"Were you?"

"Of course I was," she laughed. "I only told him because he was showing off as usual and I wanted to shut him up."

"I see," I laughed as well, half-reassured.

After school we confronted Finn together. He played a blinder. He denied saying anything to me about Emma's football tickets. He claimed they were the last thing on his mind.

He gave quite a performance, I must admit that. He even swore on his life that he hadn't said anything to me. Still, he could deny it as often as he liked, I'd heard him.

On the way home – Emma's house is on the way to mine – I said to her, "Finn's trying to cover up now by saying he didn't say anything about your tickets. Still, you know Finn, his face would explode if he told the truth."

Emma sort of laughed, then went very quiet for a moment before saying, "Everyone's been asking me about the Spurs v Arsenal match. My dad was so lucky to get tickets. People keep coming up to me saying what big Spurs fans they are and can they come with me?"

I stiffened.

"Perhaps," she went on, "I could put all their names into a hat, or maybe I should have a quiz about Spurs and let the biggest fan come with me. What do you think?"

I was too hurt to reply. What was she playing at? I was her best mate. Therefore, I should go with her. End of story. Having those tickets had really gone to Emma's head.

Well, I'd show her I wasn't bothered. I still had my amazing crystal. Emma was about to get a shock in a moment. But she wasn't the one who got the shock – it was me.

For I suddenly heard her whisper:

Finn sounded as if he was telling the truth. Did Matt make all that up about the tickets just to turn me against Finn? I think he did and I don't like that at all.

I was stunned. Not just by what Emma was saying, but the way she was speaking as if I wasn't there. Was she trying to be funny?

I turned to argue with her. She was still babbling away about how I didn't own her but her lips weren't moving.

HER LIPS WEREN'T MOVING.

In fact her whole face was completely still.

What was going on here?

The hairs rose along the back of my neck.

This was positively freaky. It was as if Emma's voice had somehow escaped from her body. I could hear it so clearly. It sounded as if she was whispering something very confidential in my ear.

Only she wasn't.

Really she was deep in thought, completely

unaware that I could hear her.

The crystal was becoming very hot now. I had to let go of it. At once, Emma's voice sprang back into her body again.

I gaped at her in amazement. My heart was beating furiously.

"What's the matter?" asked Emma. This time her lips were moving again.

"The matter," I muttered. My mouth was dry; I could hardly swallow.

"You look like you've seen a ghost ... Are you all right?"

"No, I feel a bit sick, that's all." And that was true. I felt sick with shock. "So I won't stop off at your house this evening, I'll go straight back."

Emma looked surprised. "OK ... actually you do look a bit ... rough. Are you sure you will be all right?"

"Oh yeah, say hello to Bess for me – and Finn really did say all that stuff, you know. You've got to believe me."

"Don't be silly. Of course I believe you," said Emma.

I stumbled off.

"Matt."

I turned round. Emma gave me a wicked grin. "No, I'll tell you later," she said.

I walked a few metres, but my legs felt like lead. Then I stopped. What had just happened didn't make any sense. People only spoke without moving their lips in films that hadn't been dubbed properly.

Either I was going mad or I had just made the most tremendous discovery about my crystal.

Chapter Four

Testing the Crystal

I stared down at the crystal. I hardly dared breathe on it.

Now I know what Mrs Jameson meant. It was priceless. For this crystal would let me peer into people's minds. I could discover the most top-secret information.

Actually, I already had.

Finn hadn't said a word about the Spurs tickets. He'd only thought it, and I 'overheard' him. No wonder he was so indignant.

Still, it served him right for even thinking it. And at least I knew what Finn was up to.

"I have the power to read minds," I kept muttering this over and over to myself, just as if I were casting a spell.

I still couldn't take it in.

I had to test the crystal out again. This time I decided to try it on a complete stranger.

But who?

People were walking past me too quickly and I couldn't start trailing after one of them. They'd get suspicious for a start. Then I stopped at the local sweet shop. The couple that owned it were away. I didn't know the woman who was running it for them.

I strolled inside the shop.

"Hello," I said, smiling cheerfully at the woman.

She just gave me a frosty glare in reply.

I told her what I wanted, and then I pointed my crystal towards her. The crystal quickly grew warmer. The sign that magic was about to happen. She was weighing my sweets. She didn't look up. But all at once I overheard:

Shall I wear my blue hat or my red one

to Mavis's wedding? I know the blue hat matches my jacket, but the red one is so much more expensive.

She handed me the sweets. I gave her the exact money, then said gravely, "I should wear the blue hat to Claire's wedding. It'll look so much better than the red." She looked so totally stunned I wouldn't have been very surprised if her head had started spinning.

"How do you know all this?" she managed to splutter at last.

I grinned. "Well the thing is – I know absolutely everything. Now enjoy your wedding, won't you? And in your blue hat, remember."

She didn't answer, just put out a hand as if to stop herself from falling.

Outside the shop, I laughed and laughed. The look on her face – I'll never forget that.

But it was all so incredible. One second I was just a normal kid and the next I had a superpower.

I might end up with my own TV show.

Matt the Mind Reader.

Sounds good, doesn't it? And I'd love to see

Finn's face then.

Now it was drizzling with rain. People were bustling past with shopping, rushing away. But I couldn't go home yet. I was too excited.

A guy in an expensive suit walked very slowly out of the coffee shop. He wasn't looking where he was going, bumping into people and not even noticing. He was too busy frowning hard at his mobile phone. What on earth was the matter with him?

Matt the Mind Reader will find out. I moved my crystal nearer to him and overheard:

This merger must be top secret. No one must know about it. Absolutely no one.

Then he walked briskly past me, quite unaware that I knew his big secret.

I felt about seven feet tall. This was so intoxicating.

Then I spotted a guy – only a few years older than me – hovering outside the coffee shop. He was also staring hard at his phone, lost in thought. But what about? Time to find out.

By the way, I know exactly what *you're* thinking now: How nosy is Matt?

And you know what? I totally agree with you, but I just couldn't stop myself. I was on a roll now and soon I'd picked up the boy's thoughts:

I so want to ask Holly out, but what if she knocks me back? The shame, the humiliation ...

Then the boy spotted me staring at him. "Yeah, what do you want?" he demanded rudely.

I smiled mysteriously. Then, without thinking, I blurted out, "I have a message for you."

"What are you talking about?"

I smiled even more mysteriously. "Ask Holly out and do it right now."

The boy stared at me without blinking for about ten seconds. He was extremely shocked. "Who are you?" I so wanted to say, "Matt the Mind Reader," but just stopped myself. Then he started smiling. He even gave a little laugh.

"I know exactly who you are," he declared.

The smile fell off my face. "Oh, do you?"

"You're Holly's little brother. And she's sent you with a message for me, hasn't she?" Now he was looking at me so hopefully, I couldn't disappoint him, could I?

So I said, "A-ha."

Then he started patting me on the shoulder and saying, "I really appreciate this ... sorry, what's your name? Holly did tell me, but I've totally forgotten."

"You know what, so have I," I squeaked. And he just laughed. He was so happy.

"Might see you tonight," he said.

"Yeah," I began. What was I talking about? I wasn't Holly's little brother. So what on earth was I doing? I can tell you in two words. SHOWING OFF.

"Have to go now," I announced suddenly and then tore off home.

In my bedroom, my heart was still thumping. I'd been so reckless (not to mention monumentally stupid) for drawing attention to myself. That woman in the shop could tell her friends what I'd said, while that guy will undoubtedly discover I'm not Holly's brother. And then gossip might start as people wondered how I knew all this stuff.

I must never act so foolishly again! If anyone ever found out about my crystal ... well, the world would be at my door, wouldn't it? I'd never have a moment's peace. I certainly wouldn't ever dare wear my crystal in case someone tried to steal it. I'd probably have to keep it in a vault.

Plus, if the government ever knew about it, they'd want to take it away to perform tests on it.

And only one person was going to do tests on this crystal – ME.

Chapter Five

Talking to the Dead

The next day, I bought a notebook so that I could jot down everything I discovered about my crystal. Only I decided it was too risky to refer to the crystal directly. Especially if my notebook got into the wrong hands – for example, my sister's.

So I gave my crystal a code name. I called it 'The Third Ear'.

And then I wrote down all I'd discovered about my 'third ear'. Some amazing things actually.

For instance, if I wanted to know what

someone was thinking, I just pointed my crystal in their direction and it didn't matter how far away they were.

I found that out when I was playing football. I'm not especially good at football. I just like playing it, even if I usually end up in goal. I was in goal that day. We were playing Wycliffe, the school down the road and our big rival.

I let in two goals but also made a couple of pretty good saves. So it was 2–2 when right at the end of the match, came a penalty.

Talk about pressure. Everyone was calling out things to me. But I was only listening to one voice: my crystal, which I'd tucked safely away in my pocket.

The boy was a few metres away from me. But when I tipped the crystal towards him I picked up:

I'll let their goalie think I'm going for the left corner and then do the opposite.

Of course, I dived to the right and made the most magnificent save, even if I say so myself.

My team went crazy. Someone even called me the supreme penalty saver. Best of all, Emma was watching and gave me this huge hug.

One of the best moments of my life. No question. And all thanks to my crystal. So what else could it do?

Well, it can work through glass. So I could stand by the kitchen window and pick up what my mum was thinking in the garden – and very boring it was too. But my crystal couldn't work through walls – tried this a couple of times. It didn't work on my mobile either.

So what about with animals? It would be so great if the crystal were able to pick up their thoughts. Matt: the boy who could tame any creature. I decided to test it on the cleverest dog I know, Bess. She's incredibly obedient. It's no wonder she's won so many prizes and looks certain to win tons more.

My chance came after school. I was round Emma's house. She went inside to get us some drinks. I was left in the garden with Bess. I called her over. She came bounding over at once. Then she stared up at me, her tail thumping on the grass as she wagged it vigorously. She likes me.

And when she saw the crystal, she pricked up her ears and seemed really excited. But all I could pick up was this strange whooshing noise, just like when you hold a shell up to your ear.

Later, when Bess was asleep, she started whining and shaking her legs. She was dreaming. I've always wanted to know what dogs dream about. I nudged the crystal towards her but all I got was that whooshing noise again.

It seemed the crystal only worked on humans. Then I had a crazy thought – might the crystal work on dead bodies as well as live ones?

I'd always wanted to know if we could contact the dead.

Maybe I was about to find out. I might even discover what happens after you die.

I felt a shiver pass through me.

This was getting so creepy – but fascinating.

I decided to test out my theory at the local cemetery. I went there in the early evening. I wanted it to be dark – but not too dark. It was a raw, bleak night with a chilling wind. My nose was freezing and my hand was shaking a bit. The crystal started to get warm. And that's when this very croaky, old voice started whispering in my ear.

"Are you all right?" he asked.

This was amazingly spooky. My crystal had picked up a dead man asking me how I was.

No wonder my voice trembled a bit as I replied. "I'm pretty good, thanks. How about you?" Straight away I realised that was a very stupid question. For if he was all right he wouldn't be where he was.

"I mean, I hope you are comfortable." What was I gibbering on about? Unsurprisingly perhaps, he didn't answer. But then I heard another voice – a woman's this time, announcing, "You really can't stay here."

"Oh don't worry, I just want to know what it's like where you are."

And that's when I felt a ghostly breath on my neck.

Totally freaked out now, I yelled, "Argh!" and nearly cannoned into this elderly couple, out with their Jack Russell dog, who started yapping at me very loudly.

"Sorry about that," I began. "I thought you were ..." I stopped. It seemed a bit rude to say I thought they were both dead.

The woman shook her head gravely at me. "Have you ..." her breath steamed in the cold air, "run away from home, love?"

"What ... oh yeah, that's right," I agreed quickly. "But I'm going back there right now."

Later, I wondered if I should repeat the experiment. Only I wasn't too eager to return to that gloomy old graveyard. Not on my own, anyway. Instead, I decided to test my crystal on one of the living dead – Mr Rickets, the history teacher!

Chapter Six

Amazing, Sensational News

Everyone messes about in Mr Rickets' class. It's sort of compulsory.

We used to have great paper spitball fights in his class. I'd go home with so much yucky stuff stuck to my hair. Trust parents to ruin the fun by complaining. Now teachers – and sometimes even the headmaster – patrol around outside Mr Rickets' class. They pretend they're not, but at the slightest sign of any trouble, one of them always pops in.

Mr Rickets was talking about Henry VIII that day, I think. I couldn't be completely sure as everything he says goes through my head and falls out on the other side.

I directed the crystal towards him and tuned in. Soon, this really whiny voice came through. He was moaning about how he could never engage this class's interest even though he had tried so hard. Now all he had to look forward to was his cup of coffee at break time.

It was quite sad really. The crystal was becoming hot and I was about to tune out when I heard:

So tired, and my wig's very itchy again.

His wig?

Hold the front page! Rickets wears a wig.

This was amazing, sensational news. For while we had often commented on the awfulness of Rickets' hair – it was all permed and feathery – no one had guessed that it wasn't his own.

I was so excited, I whispered the news to Emma at once. Of course I couldn't say I'd 'overheard' Rickets, so instead I claimed I'd seen the join at the back of his head.

That news went round our classroom like wildfire. Soon, everyone was studying Rickets with more attention than they'd ever given him before. Rickets gave us a small smile. He must have thought he'd suddenly become interesting.

He set us some work. We all piled up to his desk to ask him stupid questions, while scrutinising the back of his head. Then Andy Grey gave me the thumbs up – he'd spotted the join too.

I'd been proven right. Pleased by my discovery, I was eager to find out more about the wig. So at the end of the lesson I stood asking Mr Rickets about my homework while activating my crystal. I didn't pick up anything more about the wig – but I discovered there was going to be a surprise test on Henry VIII tomorrow.

Usually Rickets' surprise tests caught me out. But not this time.

On the way home I tuned in to Emma. She still hadn't offered me the other ticket for the Spurs v Arsenal match yet. I was anxious because of Finn. He'd been hanging around with Emma again today. I had heard him boasting to her about the famous people he claimed to have met. I didn't believe a word. But was he impressing Emma?

Well, I quickly discovered she wasn't thinking about Finn at all. She was worrying about her schoolwork. Her parents thought she should be getting better marks. They'd been nagging her about that and she really didn't want to let her parents down. But she was doing her best. Why couldn't they see that?

I felt very sorry for Emma. That's why I blurted out, "I've got a feeling there might be a test on Henry VIII tomorrow."

She looked puzzled. "Rickets never said anything."

"Oh, you know how he loves to give us surprise tests. There'll be a test tomorrow, you'll see."

Sure enough, next day there was a test on Henry VIII. By the following lesson, Rickets had marked the test, and guess who got top marks ... Well, in fact, Emma did. Three more marks than me. I came second. But that was cool because Emma was so happy.

The day was spoilt though by someone (I'm pretty sure it was Finn) scrawling on the board: RICKETS WEARS A WIG. Underneath, he'd drawn a cartoon of a bald man. (A two-year-old could have drawn something better.)

And of course Rickets saw it. We expected him to explode and put the whole class in detention. I wouldn't have blamed him if he'd done that. Instead, he just picked up the board rubber and erased the offending picture.

He didn't say a word either. But his eyes seemed to have closed up. And he tottered uncertainly towards his desk. I knew – without needing to consult the crystal – that he was feeling sick inside.

He had massive problems keeping classes in order anyway. Now, thanks to me, he had a fresh one – because, of course, the whole school now knew about his wig.

I felt more than a bit sick too. I'm sure I wasn't using the crystal as Mrs Jameson intended: I was acting just like a pickpocket, foraging around in people's heads and stealing their secrets. You've heard of Peeping Toms, well I was the very first

Listening Tom.

But later I changed my mind. After all, if I had supersonic hearing, you wouldn't expect me to plug up my ears every time I went out, would you?

So what's the difference with my crystal?

I did make this pledge, though. Everything I found out by 'tuning in' would remain in confidence, save for anything that might do me or my friends harm.

That was fair, wasn't it?

From now on, I was determined to use my crystal properly.

And I'd start by helping Mr Rickets.

His homework was to discover all we could about Henry VIII's six wives.

But as usual, no one bothered. I really meant to – only I totally forgot. Honestly, I did.

So when Mr Rickets started firing questions at the class, everyone just stared blankly at him. And he didn't tell us off – he never tells us off. He just stood there looking very, very disappointed.

But then I remembered my crystal. And soon I 'picked up' Mr Rickets thinking:

Surely they know Henry VIII's third wife was Jane Seymour.

I immediately called out, "Jane Seymour, sir."

"That's right. Well done, Matt," he said excitedly. "I'm glad someone did some work last night." After that I – or my crystal – was able to answer every single one of his questions. No wonder at the end of the lesson Mr Rickets gave me a big, beaming smile. He hadn't looked so happy – well, ever. But in the playground the whole class turned on me.

"You big swot," was one of the kinder things they called me.

"I just think," I replied, "Rickets could be a really good teacher – if we give him a chance and stop messing about all the time."

Everyone just gaped at me and laughed mockingly until Emma said suddenly, "Actually, I like Rickets. He never, ever shouts at us and if you ask him anything, he's dead helpful."

Soon, a few other people were murmuring their agreement, then Andy Grey said, "If Rickets gets so fed up he packs teaching in, I bet we'll have someone far worse. So I suppose we could ease up on him a bit."

Finally, over half the class decided to give Mr Rickets a 'chance'.

I was proud of myself that day and the way I'd used the crystal. And I was determined not to make any more mistakes.

But I did – a really bad one too.

Chapter Seven

End of a Friendship

On Saturday morning, I went to the Spring Fair at our school with Emma. I had to lend her ten pounds as her parents never give her much pocket money, but I didn't mind.

We were having such a great time, just messing about. But then Finn saw us and instantly killed the atmosphere stone dead.

"Is this a happening place or what? Come on, guys, fill me in on the scene?" He was trying so hard to be funny. And Emma even laughed.

He smirked at her, "You look so mint," and then actually stretched out his arm. I waited for her to tell this pain in the neck to get lost. But instead she linked arms with him. She did then turn round, smile at me and say, "Come on, Matt."

"Yeah, keep up, Spud!" yelled Finn. It seemed nothing could dent his confidence. Not even coming bottom in maths every single lesson ...

And now I was tagging after them. You're so right, I was seething – but very quietly. I didn't want Finn to know he'd got to me. Again.

Now, on one of the stalls was the largest jar of sweets I'd ever seen. Everyone was gawping at it. You could win all those sweets if you guessed correctly how many were in the jar. The guy in charge of the stall was the only one who knew the answer and everyone kept asking him for a clue. But he smiled and refused every time. Then Finn announced he knew anyway.

If he won the sweets, he'd go on about it for centuries. It would be yet another trophy for him to show off to Emma about.

I had no choice but to enter the competition too. Luckily, my crystal had 'overheard' the organiser. I knew EXACTLY how many sweets were in that jar.

And so I won, didn't I?

I strolled triumphantly around the fair with my remarkably heavy jar of sweets. A little voice inside my head wondered if I'd cheated – having inside information from my crystal. But I swept the voice away by pointing out that if I hadn't butted in, Finn would have certainly won as his guess was the nearest after mine. So you could say actually I'd saved the world from a deeply annoying event.

Plus, I shared my sweets around, which was more than Finn would have done.

Emma was dead impressed and that was really cool too. "But you guessed it exactly right. How on earth did you do that?"

"I must be a genius."

She laughed.

"And I had a secret informer."

She laughed again.

"No, I was just lucky, I suppose," I said finally.

"You've been lucky a lot recently, haven't you," said Emma. "And perhaps you'll go on being lucky," she added with a teasing smile.

She wouldn't say any more. But I took that to mean she was going to let me have that other Spurs ticket.

And about time too. I was her best friend and I had helped her get top marks in the history test. I so deserved that ticket.

But on Monday I received a big shock. I was sitting in maths with the jar of sweets beside me – I'd given away masses, but I still had hundreds left – and I was just casually tuning in to a few people, or 'surfing' as I like to call it. To be honest, it wasn't very exciting – most of them were only thinking about food – but then I directed my crystal at Finn.

I didn't enjoy tuning in to him. In fact, I hated to hear his smug voice whispering in my ear – YUCK. But I had to know what the enemy was up to.

Finn must have noticed me glancing at him because I 'overheard':

I'd hate Spud to find out and so would Emma.

Then he started thinking about something else. But, of course, it was driving me mad. What mustn't I find out? And then he caught me looking at him again and I heard:

I don't think Spud likes me very much. And if he knew Emma was coming round my house tonight ...

Then he started to laugh in his head. Horrible braying sounds, which instantly gave me a migraine.

All day I walked around in a fog of misery. But I didn't get a chance to say anything to Emma until we were walking home together.

I told myself to be calm, be cunning. So I asked as lightly as I could manage, "What are you up to this evening then?"

Emma shrugged her shoulders. "Nothing much, just do my homework and then go on YouTube. The usual." Then she quickly changed the subject.

Of course, I knew she was lying. It was becoming harder to control my anger. "I see

Finn's still creeping around you, hoping you'll give him the Spurs ticket."

Emma's face reddened.

"He's got a nerve, hasn't he, trying to steal my ticket?" I went on.

"Your ticket!" she exclaimed.

"Yes, you're going to give the other ticket to me, aren't you?"

Emma didn't say anything, just gave a strange kind of half-laugh. Was she amused? Was she starting to feel guilty?

My crystal would know.

This is what it picked up:

Just sick of Matt going on about this Spurs ticket all the time, like it's his property. Well, I'll show him. When I go round to Finn's house tonight I'll see if he wants the ticket.

I snatched my hand away from the crystal. I felt as if I'd just been punched in the stomach. I hardly spoke to Emma after that – and she hardly spoke to me either.

That evening, my head was in a whirl. I wanted to go to Finn's house — sorry, mansion — and smash all his windows. I wanted to do something bold and dramatic and nasty. I plotted all sorts of impossible things in my head.

Next morning, I arrived at school to see Emma and Finn laughing together in the playground. That's when something inside me snapped. I stormed over to Emma. "I hope you and Finn enjoy the football match together," I sneered.

Emma gaped at me in total astonishment.

"Matt ... what are you talking about?"

"I know you were round Finn's house last night," I snapped.

"How do you know?" demanded Finn at once, his face reddening. And Emma suddenly looked guilty too.

"I notice you're not denying it," I cried. "And I want the ten pounds back I lent you on Saturday. I'm always lending you stuff and not getting it back." The words leapt out of my mouth before I even realised what I'd said. I instantly wanted to snatch them back. But it was too late.

Emma was looking at me with such a shocked

and puzzled expression, as if I'd morphed into a total stranger. Then, without another word, she zoomed off.

She didn't sit with me at registration. Well, I didn't care. But at break time she was waiting for me by my locker.

She hissed. "I wouldn't have gone to that Spurs match without you, Matt. You don't know me at all, do you?" Then she thrust an envelope in my hand before storming off. I ripped it open. Inside was ten pounds and a note.

Here's the money I owe you. You've completely changed and I don't like you any more.

She'd pressed down so hard with her pen there were little tears on the paper. The words seemed to jump up and hit me in the face. I blinked furiously.

I'd totally overreacted, hadn't I? Just because you think something, doesn't mean you're going to do it. In the heat of the moment you can ponder all sorts of wild things.

Emma had no intention of really giving Finn

my Spurs ticket. I should have realised that. I'd acted without thinking. But these days I never seemed to have the time to hear my own thoughts. I was too busy listening to everyone else's. However, there was still the mystery of why she'd secretly gone to Finn's house last night.

But actually, that was no mystery. She obviously likes him and knew I'd be upset if she told me. I so wished she'd been honest with me. I'd have got used to the idea — eventually. But right now I just wanted Emma and me to be mates again.

So I tried my hardest to patch things up with her, but every single time Emma blanked me out. The following Monday, I heard her talking about the Spurs v Arsenal match. She'd gone with her cousin Giles, who I knew she didn't even like much. I blocked up my ears and whizzed away.

Soon, Emma and I got into the habit of not talking. And yeah, I hated that. You see, I missed her so much.

It was horrible, always walking home from school on my own. But I still had my trusty crystal. So every evening I went surfing – it was good fun tuning in to complete strangers. Even if most of their thoughts were dull or made no sense.

One day, I thought, I'll do this and tune in to something really bad.

That's exactly what happened.

Chapter Eight

A Terrible Discovery

It was Friday afternoon. I was trailing home. I'd tuned in to this woman who was singing to herself – a soul number that I'd never heard before – totally unaware that her song was flittering around in my head too.

But even that didn't cheer me up. All day long, my head was full of voices and I had never felt so lonely.

Then I passed Emma's house. Emma had been away ill from school for the past two days. I stopped, hoping to catch a glimpse of her. Maybe we could talk more easily out of school. I wanted this silly feud between us to stop.

I didn't see Emma, but I spotted Bess asleep in their porch. She saw me and started barking and wagging her tail. She was still my friend.

"All right, quiet now, Bess," I called through the glass. She heard me and obeyed right away. She was such a great dog.

Then I spotted this guy on the opposite side of the road. And I had the weirdest feeling that he was watching me. So I tilted the crystal towards him. He murmured in my ear:

So the family's away tomorrow. We'll grab the dog in the evening. It's very quiet round here, so it should be easy.

Then I had to let go of the crystal. By the time it had cooled down, the man was already walking away. I had to follow him to discover more.

I ran up to the top of the road. There was no sign of him. He'd vanished without trace. Maybe his car had been parked close by.

I immediately jotted down a description of

him – about forty-five or fifty, completely bald, in a smart grey suit and wearing glasses the size of a small television screen. Not the sort of person I'd imagine stealing dogs. But then I supposed dog-nappers came in all shapes and sizes.

Certainly there'd been a piece in the local paper about this gang who went around stealing dogs and demanding a ransom for them.

A shiver ran down my spine. Was this about to happen to Bess? I HAD TO DO SOMETHING. But what? My head was spinning.

I went home. Eating my meal in a kind of trance, I decided I must warn Emma. I started to send her a text but then stopped. It seemed such a crazy thing to tell her. "Hello, Matt here – just to let you know your dog is going to be stolen tomorrow. Don't ask me how I know, I just do. Have a great day, now. Bye."

It'd be much better if Emma didn't hear the news from me. I could always ring her, conceal my number and disguise my voice. I'm pretty good at acting. So I tried out this really high, ancient voice. I was quite proud of it. I sounded at least ninety-seven.

But in the end, I decided it would be simpler if I sent Emma an anonymous note.

This is what I wrote:

BEWARE, AN ATTEMPT WILL BE MADE TO STEAL YOUR DOG, BESS, TOMORROW. DO NOT LET YOUR DOG OUT OF YOUR SIGHT. GOOD LUCK.

A WELL-WISHER

I slipped out, sneaked up her drive, popped the message through her letterbox and raced home again.

I'd just got in when the phone rang. It was Emma. She was not at all happy. "Did you just send me a really stupid note?"

"Me? No," I quavered. Then I added quickly, "What note?"

"It was you, wasn't it?" she said. "You tried to disguise your handwriting, but I recognised it right off."

But how could she? It had all been in block capitals.

"I'm sorry, Emma." I was doing my best to sound utterly baffled. "I haven't a clue what—"

"Plus, I saw you," she interrupted.

"Where?" I demanded.

"Darting up my drive tonight in a highly suspicious manner."

"Oh, did you?" My voice fell. And I thought I'd been so clever.

"You'd make a terrible spy." She said this almost affectionately, but then Emma's voice rose. "You're trying to get back at me, aren't you?"

"No ..." I began.

"With a stupid little prank that isn't even funny."

"Emma, listen—"

But she rushed on. "My mum's worked up enough with all this in the local paper about dog-nappers without you making things up."

"I'm not making it up," I said. "I'm trying to warn you to keep an eye on Bess tomorrow."

"You know we're going away tomorrow."

"You are?"

"Yeah, we're off to a wedding. I told you

about that weeks ago."

She had, as it happens. But I'd completely forgotten. "So what are you doing with Bess?"

"Miss West, our next-door neighbour, is looking after her. And she used to breed dogs, so she knows how to care for them."

I pictured Miss West in my head. She hadn't lived here long and the first time I saw her I thought she had purple hair. And you know what — she had. The next time it was blue and lately it's been red. But she was a nice woman, really smiley and friendly. She was pretty old though.

"Bess could be snatched quite easily from Miss West!" I cried, "I reckon that's why they've picked tomorrow. Do all your neighbours know you'll be away tomorrow night?"

"Some do, I suppose," began Emma. Then her voice rose again. "But this is rubbish. Why are you doing all this? It's because I didn't give you my Spurs ticket. That's what this is really all about, isn't it?"

"No, no," I practically shouted. "I couldn't care less about the Spurs ticket now. I'm trying to warn you about Bess and that's all. Honestly."

Emma's voice softened slightly, "But how on earth do you know all this? You totally have to tell me."

"I heard someone plotting it," I said at last.

"What, all by himself?"

"No, no," I went on quickly. "There were two of them – two men actually."

"And what exactly did they say, these two men?"

I took a long breath. "They were in your road, opposite your house in fact – and they said, "There's a valuable dog in that house and we're going to steal it tomorrow night."

"Well they don't sound very good criminals, discussing their plans in the road for everyone to hear. I don't think we've got anything to fear from them."

There was no disguising the sarcasm in Emma's voice. "And tell me, did they carry a bag marked 'Swag' and did they—"

"Look, I wouldn't make up anything bad about Bess. You must know that," I interrupted.

"Right now, I don't think I know you at all." She sounded so sad – and then she rang off.

I wanted to ring her straight back. And for one mad moment I even wondered if I should tell her about my crystal. Anything to get her to believe me. Then I considered calling Emma's mum. But she was a very nervous, tense woman anyway. And I really didn't want to freak her out.

And maybe – just maybe – I'd misunderstood that bald-headed man. I mean, I'd only caught a snatch of his thoughts. And he really didn't look like someone who belonged to a gang of dog-snatchers.

Now what should I do? I paced around my bedroom for ages while rain splattered against the window. Then I heard loud laughter downstairs. I investigated and discovered Mum, Dad and Alison were playing cards.

Usually, Alison is out with Tony, her boyfriend. But tonight she was staying in – although Tony didn't know that – as she didn't want Tony to take her for granted.

"Let him wonder where I am," she said. "Let him worry a little bit."

Yeah, that's right. My sister's completely

cracked.

But I joined in the game of cards just for something to do really. My dad was in one of his silly moods and kept trying to sneak glances at our cards. Of course, I didn't need to do that. Instead, I set my crystal to work. Immediately, I'd 'hear' them thinking about the cards they had and what they should do next.

I won every game, didn't I?

"What's your secret, Matt?" asked Mum.

"I'm just a very skilful person, I suppose," I said. My sister made some sort of coughing laugh noise.

"Well, let's have one more game," said Mum, "and see if we can dethrone the champion."

It was going really well until I came to my sister. I turned to her and then discovered she was thinking in French. I struggled to understand, concentrating hard.

"Can't understand my French, can you?" she murmured.

"It's your rotten accent," I began.

Then I stopped and gave a gulp of sheer horror.

Alison smiled triumphantly.

My heart was now in my throat.

"Come on, you two," said Dad. "Stop staring at each other and get on with the game." I was so thrown by what had happened that I lost.

"Seems like your luck has finally run out," Dad said to me.

My sister was waiting upstairs for me. "You're either an alien, who has taken human form, which wouldn't surprise me," she said, "or you're using that crystal to read minds."

"What are you talking about?" I gasped.

"I watched you," she said. "Every time you fiddled with that crystal you picked up what cards we had. And then when I started thinking in French, you knew didn't you?" Her voice rose. "You knew!"

I started to laugh wildly. "I was only messing about …"

"No you weren't."

"Of course I was," I laughed even more wildly.

"I can always tell when you're lying," said Alison.

"I'm not lying." But I could feel my face

turning bright red.

"All right, if you won't tell me the truth I'll do this." And right then she yelled, "Mum, Dad, I've got something very important to tell you about Matt!"

I shot to my feet. "Keep your voice down."

"Why should I?" She had this really crafty smile on her face now. In the end, the only way I could quieten her down was to let her have a go with my crystal.

"I bet I can pick up your thoughts." Alison held the crystal just as she had seen me do. And she was shaking with excitement.

But then I had an idea. I'd seen a film once about these alien children who could read minds. Only, the doctor stopped them reading his thoughts by building this wall in his head.

I had to do that. Then Alison would believe my crystal couldn't do anything and my secret would be safe.

I imagined a great, high brick wall. I pictured the wall growing higher and higher. No one could ever see over the top of it. It hid everything ... everything.

Suddenly my sister let out a cry. "Ow, that crystal gets hot, doesn't it?"

"Yeah, it does sometimes." Then as casually as I could, "Hear anything, did you?"

"Yes," she said.

My heart started to thump.

"I heard this strange noise like when you put a shell up to your ear."

This was the same noise I'd heard when I tried to tune in to Bess. But she hadn't picked up anything else. And she seemed to lose interest in my crystal after that.

So my plan had worked. Still, it had been a close shave. And all because I had to show off when I was playing cards. I'm getting as bad as Finn. What a horrible thought. I was very ashamed of myself. Mrs Jameson kept the crystal's secret all her life. I nearly gave it away in less than three weeks – and to my sister, of all people!

I read Mrs Jameson's letter again. If only she'd finished it instead of putting those daft squiggles at the end. I really needed to hear her words of wisdom about the crystal. I had a horrible feeling I hadn't used it at all wisely.

That night I lay awake for ages worrying about Bess. Was she really a dog in danger? If so, I had to save her. But how? I couldn't call the police because where was my evidence? Maybe Miss West would let me look after Bess tomorrow. That was an idea. Then at least I'd know Bess was safe, as she'd be with me and I'd never let her out of my sight.

I finally fell asleep. Next morning I woke up with a start. I sensed something was wrong.

I reached out for my crystal. I always keep it on the little table by my bed.

Then my breath stopped in my throat.

It wasn't there.

Chapter Nine

The Missing Sister

I sat bolt upright up in bed and searched frantically for the crystal. It was gone – stolen.

I knew immediately who the chief suspect was.

I tore into my sister's bedroom. Normally she lolled in bed until midday on a Saturday. But not today. I raced downstairs.

"I don't believe it. Another one up early," said Dad.

"There'll be pigs flying past the window next," said Mum. They were both sitting at the kitchen table reading the news.

I burst over to them. "Alison. Where did she go?"

"Into town, I suppose," said Dad. "I told her a lot of the shops wouldn't even be open yet, but she just shot out of the door."

"You should have stopped her," I shouted, "because she's stolen my crystal!"

Both Mum and Dad gave me shocked looks.

"Alison wouldn't do that," said Mum.

"She's done it," I replied.

"Now, you go upstairs and search properly before you start making accusations like that," said Dad.

But I just knew Alison had my crystal. I thought I'd cunningly put her off the scent last night. She'd been the cunning one pretending to believe me, then sneaking into my room and nicking my precious crystal.

What was she doing with it now — testing it out on someone? Or maybe she was about to sell it? I wouldn't put anything past my sister. Fear shot through me.

I raced into town after her. It was still early, only about half past nine. And there weren't many people about. I should find my sister easily.

She was often hanging about in the town centre, sitting by the fountain.

But today she wasn't.

I spotted a few other people I knew and normally I would have chatted with them. But today I just rushed past.

I saw everyone except my sister.

She'd vanished.

She must be somewhere.

Think. Think. Think!

She might have gone to Tony's house. Maybe she was going to try the crystal out on him.

I sped off towards his house. He lived near Emma. And on the way I saw Miss West. She was taking Bess for a walk. Bess yelped excitedly when she spotted me. But Miss West didn't look very sturdy at all. Anyone could snatch Bess away from her. She recognised me.

"I'll take Bess for a walk later if you want," I said.

"That's kind of you, dear," she said, "but to be honest, I enjoy the exercise."

"Well, er, actually I could look after her all day if you like. Save you the trouble." My mum wasn't keen on dogs but I was sure she wouldn't mind just this once.

Miss West gave me a strange look. "I'm sure we'll be fine," she said firmly. I think I'd offended her. She walked away with her head raised in the air. I'll just have to keep coming back and checking on Bess.

Then I reached Tony's house. He opened the door. He gazed at me hopefully. "Have you got a message from Alison?" he asked eagerly.

"No."

His face fell.

"But she was here this morning?" I asked.

"She certainly was."

"And was she holding a keyring – with a crystal?"

"That's right." My stomach tightened. "I'd never seen it before. She said it was a present," he continued.

I smiled grimly. "And do you know where she is now?"

"I wish I did. We had this argument about – well, I haven't a clue what she was so mad about to be honest. She just started asking me if

I loved her and how much did I love her?"

Inside my head I made very loud yucking noises.

"Then I was just answering her when she went crazy and stormed off. And I didn't say anything that could have upset her. Honestly, Matt."

"No, but you probably thought something," I muttered.

"What's that?"

"Don't worry about it."

"Will you tell Alison I'm sorry for – well, whatever it is I've done wrong?"

"No way," I began, then seeing his stricken face, I relented a little. "Well, I might – but personally, I'd say you are better off without her."

So I knew she'd called at Tony's and used the crystal on him. But where was she now?

Then suddenly it didn't matter any more. For staring up at me was the crystal. It was lying on the path right by Tony's bin. Alison must have been so angry she'd flung it there. How very lucky she was a terrible shot, as I'd never have thought of looking for it in the bin.

I can't tell you how happy I was to have my crystal back. I clipped it back on my belt loop. I'd never take it off again – and somehow I would put an alarm on it.

Then I became angry. My sister had no business nicking my crystal like that and then just chucking it away as if it were an empty crisp packet.

I stormed home.

"Oh good, you've found your crystal," beamed Mum. "So where had you put it?"

"I hadn't put it anywhere," I muttered through clenched teeth. "Is Alison back?"

"Yes," Mum hesitated. "But she came home really worked up about something. You haven't been upsetting her have you?"

"Me?" I spluttered.

"Now, don't go disturbing her – you can sort out your little misunderstanding later."

LITTLE MISUNDERSTANDING.

Thanks to my devious – not to mention treacherous – sister I could have lost my most precious possession forever.

She couldn't get away with that. I hovered in her bedroom doorway, "Come on, Alison, you're not asleep."

But it seemed she really was. I stood glaring at Alison, holding my crystal triumphantly. "Yes, I got it back," I hissed. "But no thanks to you. You should never have taken it."

There was a slight pause, and then I 'overheard' Alison reply:

I know, but I thought you'd tricked me somehow. I wanted to see if it really did work.

I stared at her in amazement. Alison was still asleep. But not only was she able to hear me, I could pick up her thoughts too. Or the crystal could.

"I had to find out if Tony truly loved me," she went on, then she gave a little sob.

I stared at my sister in disgust. Fancy wasting the crystal on something so completely stupid as that.

"Then I did find out." She let out a sob. "And

I got so upset I threw it in the bin," she said.

"I know," I replied. The crystal got hot then, and while I was waiting for it to cool down, I had a brainwave. I wasn't sure if it would work, but it was worth a try.

After I'd tuned in to Alison again I said, "Repeat after me – Matt's crystal hasn't really got any special powers."

"Matt's crystal hasn't really got any special powers," she chanted.

This was totally awesome. For the first time in her life my sister was doing what I said.

"I imagined the whole thing," I continued.

"I imagined the whole thing," repeated Alison, in a dull, expressionless voice.

"Matt, what are you doing?"

I sprang round to see Mum frowning at me. "I asked you not to disturb your sister. Now you can come and help me in the garden."

I didn't have time to check whether my plan had worked. But if it had – well, that would be amazing. I could not only read minds, I could control them.

I felt suddenly flooded with magic powers,

even though I was pulling up weeds at the time.

I wanted to go back and check on Bess. But Mum kept me busy all afternoon while my sister slept on. It was after six o'clock when I finally escaped. I sped off to Miss West's house.

It was lucky I hadn't been any later, for that's when I spotted a familiar figure just ahead of me. It was the bald-headed man I'd 'overheard' plotting to kidnap Bess.

And as casually as anything, he was strolling up Miss West's drive.

Chapter Ten

Trapped

I pelted down the road.

"Miss West, look out!" I yelled.

The bald-headed man turned round.

I really thought he was going to say something to me. But instead, he quickly hurried on.

And Miss West hadn't closed her door properly. That meant Slap-Head could just walk into her house. And that is exactly what he did.

I watched with mounting horror.

This was getting worse and worse. Right now he could be tying up poor Miss West and stealing Bess. There was no time to call anyone for help. I had to do something.

So I pounded up Miss West's drive, dizzy with shock and determination. The door was still open. I stepped inside. "Miss West, it's me, Matt! Are you all right?"

The house was eerily silent. No sign of Miss West. Or Bess either. That was most unusual. Bess always springs to the front door at the tiniest sound.

I didn't like this at all. I ventured inside a little further.

"Miss West, are you …?" I began again. Then I heard a tiny sound behind me, like someone moving very stealthily. The next instant, I felt a sharp blow on the top of my head. At the very same moment, I heard someone cry out. A woman's voice. Was it Miss West? But then I felt myself falling … falling. It was like the end of a dream. Only this was real, wasn't it?

That's everything I can remember until I tried opening my eyes. Where on earth was I? I was lying on a very uncomfortable camp bed and the room still seemed to be spinning.

Somehow I scrambled to my feet, and then

immediately sagged back down again. I took some deep breaths and got up once more. I was lying in a tiny room containing nothing but that camp bed, a cracked wardrobe and a peculiar smell. A dead musty, jumble-sale stench.

I staggered over to the window and immediately recognised Miss West's back garden. Emma's football had an annoying habit of landing there. So I was upstairs in a sort of boxroom. I stumbled to the door. It wouldn't open. It was locked from the outside.

I half ran to the window again. It was locked too – and double glazed.

I was trapped. I wondered where Miss West was now. I shivered.

In the garden, Bess was lying on the grass, panting. But then I watched Slap-Head coming over to her with a ghastly smile on his face and waving this meat in his hand that had to be laced with some kind of sleeping pill. As soon as Bess had eaten it, he could carry her away.

Bess was edging nearer to the meat now. I guess the smell was irresistible.

Thick hedges grew on either side of the

garden. No one else could see what was going on. Only me.

I rattled as hard as I could on the window. I yelled out. But the glass was thick and all Bess's interest was focussed on the meat. She was sniffing it now.

In a moment I'd have to watch Bess fall to the ground and that man sneak away with her. I might never see Bess again. She could be sold to someone thousands of miles away.

My eyes blurred.

I twisted my crystal around in frustration. Inside my head I screamed:

Bess, that meat is bad. You mustn't eat it. Do you understand? It's bad!

I let go of the crystal. At the same moment Bess stopped and turned her head on one side. She always does that when she's puzzled. It was just as if she'd heard me. But that was impossible. I'd tested the crystal on Bess and hadn't picked up anything.

But, boil my brains, I hadn't thought of the

other possibility. What if Bess could hear my thoughts? After all, dogs can hear many sounds that we can't.

I grabbed the crystal again and waited for it to become warm. The next few seconds lasted forever.

Then I saw Bess pick up the poisoned meat. The world froze. She flopped down on the grass, all set for a good feed. I held the crystal even tighter. I let the heat flow through my fingers. Then I sent this urgent message to Bess:

Drop the meat. It's not good for you. Drop the meat.

Again she cocked her head to one side. She could hear me all right. But she wasn't very keen to obey me.

Emma and I were always telling her to drop things she found in the garden. She had a special fondness for forget-me-nots even though they always made her sick. When she didn't want to drop something, Bess would lower her head and grip whatever it was more tightly. She was doing it now.

Bess, drop it! Drop it now.

Inside my head I was shouting at the top of my voice. My lips started moving too – even though no sound came out of them.

All at once Bess did drop the meat and then she began wagging her tail as if to say, "Haven't I been a good girl?"

Slap-Head bent down beside her. I guessed he was talking to her, urging her to eat the meat.

The crystal had become scorching hot. My whole body screamed with the pain. But I daren't let go of it now.

Well done, Bess, now run away from the man. Run away.

Bess obeyed this instruction at once. I don't think she cared much for Slap-Head anyway. She started bounding about the garden.

Good girl, keep running. Don't let him

catch you.

We sometimes played tag with Bess and it was a game she loved. Perhaps she thought she was playing it now as she went leaping through the flowerbeds.

Then she stopped and looked around her, as if she was trying to work out where I was hiding. Slap-Head didn't try to follow her. He just stared in bewilderment.

He must have thought Bess had gone mad. He picked up the meat and began calling to her again. But she just hid behind the tree for a moment, then started racing all round the garden again.

The crystal slipped from my fingers. I couldn't hold it any longer. My hands had turned red and they felt as if they were covered in wasp stings.

But what did that matter? Bess was safe – for now, anyway. And actually, my fingers seemed to recover remarkably quickly.

The doorbell rang. The ringing vibrated through the whole house. I sprang to the bedroom door and yelled, "Help. I'm trapped in here. Help!"

I've never shouted so loudly in my life – well, not since I was a screaming baby, anyway. But my only reply was a deafening silence.

They must have gone away, whoever they were. I pounded on the door in total frustration.

Suddenly I froze. I could hear another sound – a clicking and creaking noise. I recognised it too. It was the sound of Miss West's back gate. And the next moment, I saw Emma and her parents peering all round the garden.

I actually rubbed my eyes. I wasn't hallucinating, was I? Slap-Head looked totally amazed too. He dropped the meat and stood as still as a marble statue. Bess bounded over to Emma and her parents, madly excited to see them. Then she began tearing around the garden again. She was determined to play tag with someone today.

Slap-Head was speaking to Emma's parents, desperately trying to talk his way out of the situation. I wondered what lies he was telling them. But Emma's parents looked very suspicious. I guessed they were asking where Miss West was.

Meanwhile, I was pounding away at the window. And finally Emma looked up and saw me.

Chapter Eleven

Another Shock

"It was very clever of Bess not to eat the meat," said Emma. "Do you suppose she somehow knew it was poisoned?"

"Of course she did." I patted her head. "She's an amazing dog." I looked at Emma. "It was just so lucky you turned up when you did."

"Well, all day I was thinking about what you said and I didn't think you'd just make that up – not about Bess. You care about her nearly as much as I do."

I nodded vigorously.

"And then some of your other predictions

have come true," continued Emma. "So I pretended my tummy bug had come back, and that I wanted to come home. How are you feeling now?"

"Just great," I said at once. It had been twenty minutes since I'd been let out of the bedroom and actually I still felt a bit shaky. Miss West had also been tied up and was very agitated. She sat drinking a cup of tea while Emma's parents interrogated Slap-Head. They had already phoned the police.

He wasn't saying much, although I could see little purple veins pulsing on his head. In a low, dry voice he told how he'd just happened to spy Bess and thought he could get a good price for her. But somehow his story didn't quite ring true – not to me, anyway – and why the heck was he confessing? Something just didn't add up.

"How did you know we would be away?" asked Emma's mum.

"I overheard people talking in one of the local shops," he replied vaguely.

Then the police arrived and said they'd take Slap-Head in for questioning. Emma's parents had to go with them to the police station too, while Emma and I stayed behind to comfort Miss West.

We sat chatting about what had happened and, half by accident, I tuned in to Miss West. That's when I picked up something truly incredible:

This was such a mistake. I should never have let him talk me into this. Why do I always listen to my brother?

Slap-Head was her brother?

Did that mean Miss West was in on the plot too? Surely not. Miss West was nice — and she had a blue rinse, for goodness' sake. It was very hard to believe, or prove.

Then I had a brainwave. In the corner on the wall there were some old black-and-white photographs. I got up and studied them carefully. Surely if Slap-Head was her brother, he'd be in one of these snaps. It took a while, but I found one. He had a full head of hair then.

I nodded to Emma to come over. Looking a bit

puzzled, she got up. I pointed at the photograph. "Who does that remind you of?"

Emma saw at once. She rounded on Miss West. "That man who was here, you know him. He's a relation of yours, isn't he? You're both in on this together."

All the colour left Miss West's face. "My photographs," she whispered. "We never thought of that." Then she admitted Slap-Head was indeed her brother.

"What were you going to do to Bess?" asked Emma. "Kidnap her and make us pay a ransom, or maybe you were going to kill her?"

"No, no," cried Miss West. "You mustn't believe that."

"I'd believe anything of you now," said Emma bitterly.

"You must let me tell you the truth," begged Miss West.

The truth was this — her brother was a dog breeder and he seemed all set to win a major prize with one of his dogs the following month. He'd never won such an important prize before. There was only one obstacle in his way — Bess.

So the plan was to make it look as if Bess had been kidnapped when Miss West was looking after her.

"But honestly, truly," cried Miss West, "she'd have been safe with my brother's other dogs, and well looked after too. And as soon as the competition was over she'd have been returned to you, safe and in the best of health."

"Thanks so much," murmured Emma with heavy sarcasm. "So just for a pathetic prize you'd inflict all this harm and upset on an innocent dog, give me and my family a truly horrible few days – and hit poor Matt over the head!"

"That really wasn't meant to happen." Miss West's shoulders sank lower and lower. "It's just Matt turned up so suddenly my brother totally overreacted." She turned to me. "But why were you here?"

"Well, er …"

"You knew something, didn't you? But how did you know?"

"I'd noticed your brother hanging around," I began, "and just got such a bad feeling—"

"And thank goodness you did," interrupted

Emma.

Miss West's mobile rang. She answered in a voice little more than a whisper. Then she stared gravely at us. "The police want me to go to the station and make a statement." I couldn't help feeling the tiniest bit sorry for her.

"And your parents are on their way back," she said to Emma. "I'll just go and get ready."

She shuffled away upstairs. Emma was now looking right at me. "If it hadn't been for you, poor Bess would now be far away." She shuddered then went on, "I'd be certain you were psychic if it weren't for one thing."

"And what's that?"

"How could you ever think I'd give my other Spurs ticket to Finn instead of you?"

"You'd never believe me," I murmured.

"Well, you got some wrong information there," said Emma firmly. "Finn isn't a real Spurs fan like you."

"But you did go round his house," I burst out suddenly.

Emma blushed and looked away for a moment. "Matt, can you keep a secret?"

"Yeah sure," I replied in the flattest voice imaginable. You see, I knew what she was going to tell me. Finn is her boyfriend. Only they don't want anyone to know yet.

I'd give anything not to hear Emma tell me that. But just because she was my best friend, didn't mean I owned her. And somehow I had to fix my face so I even looked a bit pleased, as that's what friends do, isn't it?

"The thing is, Matt ..." She looked so embarrassed.

Here it comes, I thought. Fake smile at the ready.

"I'm helping Finn do his maths homework."

I gaped at her. "But why on earth are you doing that?"

"Because I felt sorry for him always coming bottom of the class and so hating it. He says he wants to hang his head in shame every time ..."

"Finn does?" I was amazed. "I didn't think anything bothered him. He's such a total bighead."

"That's all an act," said Emma "Only he doesn't want a single person to know I'm helping him. You will keep his secret, won't you?"

"Of course I will." I was practically shaking with relief. *And you won't need my crystal to know why.*

"I always meant for you to have the other ticket, Matt. I was only teasing you. But it all went wrong. And besides, you changed so much."

"No I didn't."

"You so did. You never seemed to listen to me any more for a start. You were always far away." Her voice rose. "It was horrible, it was like you'd been bewitched. You just weren't yourself."

"Well, I'm back now."

"About time," said Emma. Then she added, "The Spurs v Arsenal match wasn't so great." A little smile crossed her face. "I think next Saturday's match will be much better."

"So do I." I grinned.

Then I had to go to the doctor's for a check-up. Even though I said I felt fine.

Before I left, Miss West came downstairs to say goodbye. She apologised to both of us again. She even bent down and whispered sorry to Bess. She looked terrible – like a ghost.

She suddenly turned back to me and said, "That crystal you're wearing, Matthew. Excuse me for asking, but it reminds me very much of a crystal a friend of mine wore. I always admired it so. Her name was Mrs Jameson."

That gave me a start.

"It is Mrs Jameson's," I said slowly. "She left it to me in her will."

"Well, fancy that. A long time ago, she and I worked together - for nearly six years, you know. We were both secretaries, only she was much better than me. I could never read my shorthand back. She was always having to help me. It was such a shock when she left, and so suddenly too. Just marched out one day …"

It was then an idea sneaked into my head.

An incredible idea.

Chapter Twelve

MindReader Boy

I had to wait until Monday before I could see if I was right.

I was bursting with impatience.

But after school I tore into the library. I stayed there until the library closed at six o'clock. I knew my mum would be cross. but I couldn't move until I'd read every word of Mrs Jameson's message.

At last I'd cracked the code and I'm sure you've guessed it as well. That's right, Mrs Jameson had ended her message to me in shorthand. Armed with a shorthand dictionary,

I decoded:

Time is short and this is top secret but I know you will break my code easily.

I felt a real mouse-brain when I read that. The message continued:

I must tell you that my crystal has never brought me any happiness. I used it on the man I loved, my friends at work, and ended up a very sad, lonely woman. That is why I hesitate to give my crystal to you. Yet I know, if used wisely, it can be wonderful too. I think you are the one to discover its power for good. Goodbye.
 Your friend,
  Margaret Jameson.
P.S. There was only one person I never used the crystal on — and that was you, Matt.

I read her words over and over until I knew them by heart — Mrs Jameson's secret message to me.

She said the crystal lost her all her friends.

Well, it nearly lost me my friendship with Emma. And my sister almost broke up with her boyfriend.

Did I tell you my sister apologised to me? Earth shattering or what? It was after I got home on Saturday night. She told me she'd thought my crystal could read minds.

"But your crystal hasn't really got any special powers. I'd imagined the whole thing." Her exact words. So I really had hypnotised her when she was asleep.

That should have made me feel very happy.

After all, I could hypnotise my sister again. She would have to obey my every thought. It sounded good at first. But I didn't want to turn anyone into my puppet, not even Alison. That would be seriously spooky.

So was Mrs Jameson's letter.

She was telling me the crystal had turned her into a kind of freak.

And the same could happen to me.

That's why I put the crystal away in my cupboard. And that's where it stayed for a whole ten minutes.

Then I saw Emma coming along the road with Bess. They were calling for me. Emma looked so happy. But if it hadn't been for the crystal ... well, Bess would be far away now.

I took the crystal out of the cupboard again.

I decided I couldn't keep it hidden away. What a waste. But I'd make up a new rule.

Rule One – never use it on my family and friends.

Would you believe, I've kept that rule for one whole week.

Not that I haven't been tempted. You see, it's my birthday next month and I'm mad keen to know what my mum's bought me.

My hand's certainly twitched a few times.

But I was strong.

From now on I'll only use my crystal for good things, like solving mysteries and saving people – and animals. For with great power comes great responsibility – as Spider-Man's Uncle Ben once said.

And what's good enough for Spider-Man is good enough for MindReader Boy.

Don't worry, I'm not really going to call

myself that. But if I can ever help you, remember there's no need to text or phone – just send a few thoughts my way.

I'll be listening.

About Pete Johnson

Pete's favourite subjects at school were English and history. His least favourite was maths.

He has always loved reading. When he was younger, Pete would read up to six books a week – even more in the school holidays!

His most favourite book as a child was *One Hundred and One Dalmatians*. He wrote to the author, Dodie Smith, and she encouraged him to become a writer.

Other childhood favourites include *The Witches* by Roald Dahl, *Tom's Midnight Garden* by Philippa Pearce and Enid Blyton's *The Mystery of the Invisible Thief*.

When he was younger, Pete used to sleepwalk. One night, he woke up in his pyjamas walking along a busy road.

He has a West Highland terrier called Hattie.

His favourite food is chocolate. He especially loves Easter eggs!

Pete loved to watch old black-and-white movies with his dad on Saturday night and used to review films on Radio 1. Sometimes he watched three films in a day! Pete has met lots of famous actors and collects signed film pictures.

He likes to start writing by eight o'clock in the morning. He reads all his books out loud to see if the dialogue sounds right. And if he's stuck for an idea, he goes for a long walk.

Wherever he goes, Pete always carries a notebook with him. "The best ideas come when you're least expecting them," he says. Why don't you try that too? Maybe you'll have a brilliant idea for your own book!

To find out more about Pete and his books, go to:

www.petejohnsonauthor.com

A Note from Pete

I really hope you had fun sharing Matt's first adventure with the magic crystal.

There are some books that you really want to talk about with your friends. I'd be thrilled if this was one of them. Are you a member of a book club? I've visited several of them and they are brilliant fun. Or maybe you might want to start one of your own.

So here are a few suggestions of what to think about, just to get you started. (Of course, you don't have to be in a book club – you can do it just for fun!)

"If I could have a superpower, reading minds is the one I would choose. That was my original inspiration for the book." Pete Johnson
- Which superpower would you choose to have

- and why?
- Brainstorm what you think would be the advantages and disadvantages of having a superpower.
- How much do you believe it would change your life?

Mrs Jameson says Matt's crystal is "priceless".
- Matt thinks if the government ever found out about his crystal they'd take it from him to perform tests on it. Do you agree?
- Would you like having something so precious, or would it scare you?
- Would you carry the crystal around with you like Matt, or would you hide it away?

How does Matt use the crystal?
- Look especially at the scenes with Mr Rickets.
- When Matt discovers a secret about his teacher, he tells everyone. Was he right to do this? What would you have done?
- How does Matt try to put things right?
- When would you use your crystal at school?
- Would you ever use it on a teacher?

Matt and Emma
Matt uses his crystal on his good friend, Emma. By doing this, does Matt betray Emma?
- Do you think the crystal helps or hinders Matt's friendship with Emma?
- How would you feel if you discovered a friend 'eavesdropping' on your thoughts?
- Discuss the rule Matt makes about the crystal in Chapter Twelve.

"Humour creeps into everything I write." Pete Johnson
- Although it is not a comedy, there is humour in this story. Which part made you laugh?
- Look, for instance, at how Matt uses the crystal in the shop (Chapter Four) and the graveyard (Chapter Five).

Surprises in the story
- Readers have especially enjoyed the twists and turns in this tale. When Matt's crystal is missing, did you guess who had taken it?
- Were you shocked when you discovered the truth about Miss West?

- What was the biggest surprise in the story for you?
- Do you like books that keep you guessing?

What did you most enjoy about MindReader: The Crystal?
- The book has been described as 'exciting and funny'. Do you agree?
- Which scenes did you find the most engrossing?
- Do you think it would make a good TV series?
- Would you like to read more about Matt and his magic crystal?

You own the crystal for a day ...
- Matt lends you his crystal for a whole day with just one instruction – you must not tell anyone about the crystal's special power.
- Who would you use the crystal on – family, friends, strangers? Discuss your reasons.
- How would you feel about owning the crystal for a day? Could you keep the crystal's secret?

Read all the MindReader adventures!

978-65-86106-00-8

It's me – Matt, MindReader Boy. I have this INCREDIBLE crystal that I can use to read minds. No, really, I do! Sounds a bit like a SUPERPOWER, doesn't it?

I've had to keep it secret from everyone – even my best friend, Emma. But now I've finally told her… WHAT a mistake! But while I try to clean up THAT mess, my powers are put to a real test – only I'm rubbish at being brave! Could I REALLY be a superhero…?

Read the final MindReader mystery!

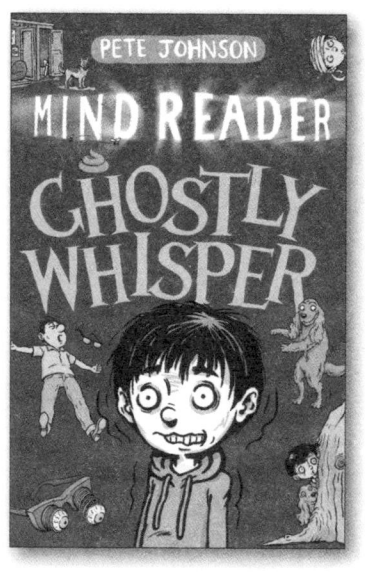

978-65-86106-07-7

Me again – Matt the mind reader. Quick, listen up, I haven't much time!

I've had some fun since I got this AMAZING mindreading crystal – chasing off burglars, saving dogs, and even becoming a superhero. But now things are getting SERIOUS. I was in the middle of solving a mystery when the crystal picked up a truly terrifying message: YOU ARE IN GREAT DANGER – WATCH OUT! Like I said, things have got serious – DEADLY serious…

Also by Pete Johnson...
Meet the hilarous schoolboy stand-up comedian, Louis the Laugh!

978-65-86106-02-2

When his dad becomes a stay-at-home parent, Louis's life is turned upside down. Faced with inedible cooking, Post-it Notes telling him to clean his room and a dad who suddenly has far too much time on his hands, Louis decides his dad must be stopped. But how?

Louis the Laugh returns!
The brilliantly funny sequel to
My Parents Are Driving Me Crazy

978-65-86106-03-9

How can you escape when you're trapped in a technology time warp? When Louis's parents decide he spends too long "glued to screens" they come up with their worst idea ever – a total ban on tablets, computers and mobiles! Louis needs a plan –and fast!

Also available:
The fiendishly funny final chapter of Louis the Laugh's awesome adventures!

978-65-86106-05-3

What can you do when your parents turn into supervillains? When Louis is caught napping in class, his mum and dad ban him from appearing on his favourite vlog. With his celebrity ambitions at stake, Louis's best friend, Maddy, tells him a way to get his parents to agree to anything…